MOON~~LIT~~

CHRISTMAS

&

OTHER

STORIES

ACKNOWLEDGEMENT

The following Authors contributed to making this book a reality and they are:

1. Victoria Olasegha
2. Emmanuel Onimisi
3. Funom Makama
4. Leke Amoo
5. Adebola Adisa
6. Niyi Marcus
7. Kayode .O. Sinmidele Valentine
8. Obiora Oji
9. Oluwaseyi Adebola
10. Victoria Ozidu
11. Ejiro Eyaru
12. Jinmi Adetutu

Special acknowledgement also goes to the families and friends of the Authors for their patience, love and understanding.

<u>*DEDICATION*</u>

This book is dedicated to all children around the world whose eyes light up at Christmas as the nighttime skies are lit with stars.

We present to you this little piece of magic wrapped in words, told with African drums, and filled with love, laughter and family.

From the bottom of our hearts…and pens, we wish you a resplendent, colourful and dazzling moonlit Christmas.

ISBN: 9798761437807

TABLE OF CONTENTS

A Family Christmas

by Victoria Olasegha

It's the Christmas season, a time when family should be together. That is what Daddy told you would happen this Christmas and you strongly agreed with all your heart. You remember what happened three years ago, when Daddy took you and your siblings, Anna, and Peter, to the village where you stayed with Grandma.

Even though Grandma couldn't see your lovely faces, and aunties and uncles you didn't know kept coming by the minute to pay their respects to her, and there was no electricity, and the smell of firewood was always in your nostrils, you had a very enjoyable Christmas. Your uncle was also in the village and between him and Daddy; they decided to give the whole village a treat by hosting a party. Daddy spent a lot of money and uncle kept telling him that he needed more money to buy more palm wine. You didn't understand why palm wine was so important and why you were not allowed to drink it.

The village party was held the day before Christmas. It started badly because the cooks that Daddy hired failed to show up and then Mummy who was unprepared, had to be drafted into cooking for nearly a hundred people. You wanted to play but you were sent by Mummy many times to fetch water and to chop this and that. It was even more annoying because Hannah and Peter could not help as they were too young.

At eight years old and being the firstborn, you were regarded as the responsible one. You were happy, however, that Mummy was cooking because you knew her rice was the best. Cooks were few but it turned out there were servers aplenty. The party was a huge success though Daddy and Mummy ended up not eating because it seemed the village just kept multiplying and the food was not enough.

Daddy was in a bad mood for a while because he did not drink the palm wine even after spending so much money. Uncle just threw up his hands and said the palm wine finished very fast. For about one week, Daddy was very careful around Mummy for two reasons and could not look her in the eye. Firstly, because in Mum's eyes was clearly written: 'I told you so.' Secondly, Daddy's eyes were still smarting from the smoke of the firewood that was burnt in the village.

After that year, Daddy decided that going to the village to spend Christmas was too expensive. So, he invited some uncles and aunts that lived close by instead. The house quickly filled up with relatives. They decided to spend not just Christmas but to see the New Year with your family. Daddy was horrified because they brought all their children. He didn't know they were so many.

You had to share your bed with them, and it wasn't easy because you loved your bed so much. The children ranged between two and six. They seemed to like visiting the toilet all the time and they were good at making a lot of mess on the floor. Your parents could hardly wait for the holidays to be over, and neither could you. You just wanted your house and your parents all to yourself. So, Daddy decided that he would not be inviting family over for Christmas next time. The rest of the family was in total agreement with that.

Last year, Daddy decided that it was high time your family were hosted for a change. He said that this will give Mum a break from cooking for all the festivities. You felt very happy because you would spend Christmas at your cousin's house. Jide was nearly your age, and you always had a lot of fun playing Game Boy together. Daddy bought everyone a set of

Christmas clothes and then drove for two hours to your cousin's house. Everyone was happy. It felt like Daddy made the best decision this time.

You and your family were treated like royalty. You had a lovely time with your cousin and thoroughly enjoyed the food: *pounded yam* and *egusi* with lots of meat that was placed in front of you. Mum hardly gave you that much meat at home. It was hard when the time came for your family to leave. Jide was nearly crying, and it seemed like sand must have gotten into your eyes as well.

On the way home, your stomach started cramping. It was so painful. By the time you got home, everybody had to take turns using the toilet, including Mummy and Daddy. You had to do 'number two' up to six times that night and it was worse for Hannah and Peter. Never again! Daddy declared. You couldn't agree more.

So, this year, Daddy decided not to make any plans. No outings. No travelling. Daddy decided to spend Christmas at home with the family – yes, with nuclear family only. He said he didn't care what grandma would say or what your uncles or aunts would say. He said the family would just have a Christmas tree, exchange presents and eat your rice in peace. You can't wait to see how that will turn out. This was probably going to be the best Christmas ever!

Dayo and the Legend of the Christmas Chicken by Emmanuel Onimisi

"There's a *chicken zombie* out there and it's *chasing me!*"

Trust me, this was not the weirdest thing we heard at Christmas that year. But when it comes to the many Christmas seasons of my childhood, this story would become my most memorable.

Christmas at Grandma's house was something we always looked forward to all year. Families from as far as Kaduna in the North and Port Harcourt in the deep South would converge at her house in Ibadan, located in the West.

The family home was in a neighbourhood far removed from the hustle and bustle of the highway and business thoroughfare most of us were used to, so Christmas with the family was always a quiet vacation for us all.

For me, Christmas was the one time I got to see my cousins, but with each new year, there was less and less to look forward to. You see, for a very long time, there had been an age gap between me and the rest of my cousins as they were all in high school when I was just learning to walk.

It was awesome then because I was the youngest and everyone pampered me. But as the years went by, a newer generation of cousins barely out of kindergarten took over my baby-of-the-house throne. So now I was stuck in that weird position with no one in my preteen age group and all my cousins either too old to play with me or so young that they were my responsibility.

That was why, that Christmas season, I spent much of my time by myself and away from the others unless it was necessary. I had no game consoles and Mum had explicitly banned me from playing games on her phone, so I spent my afternoons counting the dots in the asbestos ceiling of my room, contemplating eternity or whatever existential concepts floated in my bored mind.

On Christmas Eve (a day Uncle Gbade always called 'Christmas *Adam*', to everyone's chagrin) Ronke, the youngest of my older cousins poked her head into my room. "Come downstairs," she said. "We're preparing the chicken today."

Ronke was the closest thing to a big sister that I had. She was already in her third year at the university and spent more time on her phone these days.

I didn't budge. "Nah, thanks. I don't know how to prepare chicken."

She wasn't amused. "There's always a first time," she said. "Get up!"

I sat up, contemplating the fact that she was serious. "But I don't *want* to kill a chicken." I folded my hands in protest.

Ronke squinted at me, incredulous at what I'd said. "OK. I'll just tell Grandma that you're being stubborn." And with that, she walked away.

Grandma had always been looking for ways to keep me busy, and I had cooperated for the most part. I had helped with the dishes and tidied the house, but there were certain lines I would never cross. I loved eating chicken, but I had never even considered how the chicken got on my plate in the first place. But if Grandma heard that I was disobeying her order, I wouldn't hear the last of it.

So, I bolted after Cousin Ronke. "No, wait! Wait for me!" I sure did not need Grandma reporting me to my parents for being stubborn. They had inventive ways of disciplining me, and this holiday was enough punishment already.

Little did I know that a fate worse than punishment lay ahead of me – A family parliament.

If you don't have a big family, you might not understand what a family parliament is like. Have you ever been summoned by a teacher to the Staffroom to receive your punishment when suddenly, all the teachers begin talking about you in the third person for what seems like an eternity? Right in your presence! If hell is worse than that, then I don't want to go to hell.

A family parliament is ten times worse than this.

As I charged after Ronke I walked into the living room, where Grandma was picking vegetables by the dining table, deep in discussion with her daughters. My uncles were watching a football game on the TV, and the younger ones were playing tag nearby. Grandma's eyes lit up at the sight of me. "And guess who gets to kill our chicken for us today!" she exulted.

All eyes turned on me. All except my Mum, who chose to focus on the vegetables she was picking. Oh, she was an accomplice to all of this.

"But I don't want to!" I said. It didn't help that my voice cracked and came out as a whine.

Uncle Gbade guffawed at that. "I killed my first chicken when I was 8! You better act like a man—"

"Eh-eh," my Mum retorted at that, and for a moment I was glad she was defending me. "Don't impose your toxic expectations of masculinity on my boy. Killing chickens doesn't make him a man."

Now I wished she hadn't tried to defend me.

"Don't spoil my grandson, Funke," Grandma replied, slamming the table. "Dayo is a big boy. What is there in killing a small chicken?"

"I'm not spoiling him, Mama. He hasn't done it before…"

And there it began, everyone discussing me as if I wasn't even there. Oh, I wished the ground would just swallow me whole. Just then I noticed Ronke smirking at me from the kitchen window. At that moment, I knew that following her would be a much better fate than remaining at the family parliament.

"God forbid! No grandson of mine would be a vegetarian!" I don't even know how Grandma got to that point, but I was out of there as fast as my legs could carry me.

Ronke chuckled. "Let's stay a little longer," she said. "It was just getting fun."

I gave her a look. "Let's just get this over with."

Why's chicken important to Christmas anyway? I wondered. *Would anyone die if they didn't eat chicken? Did people have to kill chickens to eat them? How did chicken killers even live with themselves, knowing they had committed poultry homicide?*

"It's not fair," I muttered.

"Nothing ever is," Ronke said dismissively, picking up a knife and filling the bowl with water.

"Why do we have to kill chickens? Why don't we just buy them from the supermarket?"

Ronke handed me the bowl of water and opened the door to the backyard. "Are you kidding? Even the frozen ones you buy from the market didn't just freeze to death."

"At least someone else killed them."

"What happens when you're older and your family is at home for Christmas. How would you get your Christmas chicken?"

I thought about that for a second. "We won't eat chicken, then."

"Ok, what If you're stuck on an island and a chicken is the only thing you've got around. How would you survive?"

"I … I won't be stuck on an island. I'd swim away."

"What if there are sharks in the water?"

"You're not getting me to change my mind. I'm not going to kill that chicken."

By this point, we were approaching the big, fat white hen that was lying on its side by the wall, tied at its legs. It stared up at us as we approached. Quiet, despite the fate that awaited it.

"I mean, just look at it," I said. "You want me to commit murder?"

By now Ronke was weary of my banter. "Look, it's either you get back to the family court and-"

I held up my hands. "OK! Fine! Let's just do it." Ronke smiled. "You should see your face right now."

"Not helping!"

"I know." And in one swoop, she picked up the chicken by its wings as if it was the easiest thing. "Here, hold it."

I was still wondering how she did that, and how she expected me to touch it. "Really? Just like that?"

"Just like this."

I still preferred not to touch it, but then I did. The bird didn't protest as much as I expected. With shaking hands, I held it by the wings. "See," Ronke intoned. "It doesn't bite."

She dug a small hole in the ground with the tip of the knife and then rinsed it afterwards. "It's for the blood to flow when we're done. Ok, now place the chicken near the hole."

"I can't do this."

"Yes, you can. Place your left leg on the wings like this, and your right leg on the legs. Just like that. Aha. See, that wasn't so hard, now, was it?"

She showed me how to hold its head and place the knife at the right spot. "You do realise that you're teaching me how to behead, right? This should be a crime."

"Says the boy that's been eating chicken for years."

"That doesn't make it right!"

"Hey, keep your feet firm. You don't want it running away."

"I'm just saying. Someday the chickens may revolt against humanity for our crimes against their kind. I don't want to be on the wrong side of history on that day."

Ronke shook her head. "You've seen too many movies, Dayo."

"I'm sorry, Clucky," I said. "It's not my fault."

Ronke arched a brow. "Who's Clucky?"

"That's her name."

"You gave it a *name?* Just now?" Ronke chuckled. "Dude, you're something else."
"Hey, let me get through this my way, OK?"
"Ok, you do you. Dramatic much?"

I don't remember the actual moment when I finally did it, but I remember shutting my eyes and apologizing to Clucky with every swipe of the knife. It was over before I knew it, the head in one hand and the rest of the body in the other. Clucky still shook intermittently, and I couldn't help but think I had just committed murder.

Ronke, my accomplice in this homicide, patted my shoulder. "Well done, cuz. Now-"
And then everything changed suddenly in a flurry of feathers. Before our very eyes, Clucky jerked out from under my feet and sprang to its feet, flapping its wings furiously. I screamed and bolted as fast as I could away from it. My sudden fear was only further enhanced when I took another glance behind me.
A headless chicken was chasing me!

My shriek sounded like it was coming from outside of me as I rushed through the backdoor and slammed it shut behind me, to the concern of everyone in the living room beyond. And that's when awash with adrenaline, the iconic line that I would never live down for many Christmases hence was uttered from my lips.

"There's a *chicken zombie* out there and it's *chasing me!*"

I had not even thought of Ronke's safety. I had just incurred the wrath of a chicken and it was after me. That was all that mattered in those moments.

It took a couple of minutes of my family soothing me before I could calm down enough to show them the monster outside. Ronke was still alive, and she was on her knees, laughing if you can believe it. She had slammed the large bowl over the chicken. Good for her.

I would later learn that some chickens can still have enough energy to fight in their last moments and that this one escaped because the hold of my feet on its wings and legs was loose. But what did I care? This gave me some respite as I was allowed to go off by myself to rest, away from all this chicken drama and the long discussions and laughs that followed.

I barely spent a moment in the room when Ronke came by to see how I was doing. I could tell she was trying her best not to laugh in my face one more time.

"I'm never killing a chicken *ever again!*" I muttered.

She sat beside me, giggling as she did. "You don't mean that."

"Why do we have to kill chickens anyway?" I asked. "What does that even have to do with Christmas?"

She thought for a moment. "Apart from the fact that they make for a delicious meal."

"We could always have something else," I muttered.

She placed a hand on my shoulder. "When our parents were younger, they did not get to eat chicken very often. There were no KFCs or supermarkets like there are today. Christmas was the one time they got to eat something different. That's why it's become a tradition that stuck. Some family traditions will just never die."

"And we have to still suffer because of that? It's not even what Christmas is about."

She nodded. "Tell me, then. What *is* Christmas all about?"

I shrugged. "Jesus? It's about Jesus, like when He came as a baby."

"Awesome. And do you know why He came?"

I thought about it too. "To die for our sins. Not as a baby, but when He was more grown-up."

"Exactly. To take up the punishment we deserved for our sins."

"But what does that have to do with the chicken?"

"Oh, it doesn't. Not really. But every time we have Christmas chicken, knowing the little creature gave its life for our delicious meal, we can think of the sacrifice Jesus made by giving His life for us so that we could receive God's awesome gift. His gift of forgiveness and eternal life."

I sighed. "Well … yeah. I guess. But it's not the same."

She shrugged. "Hey, I'm trying to help here."

"Sorry." I smiled despite myself. "Thanks."

She smiled. "But you do know that the 'chicken zombie' line is legendary now, right."

I buried my face in my hands. "Oh … please don't remind me."

"Yep. It will be passed on for generations, how the Mighty Dayo was almost vanquished by a chicken."

"Please stop…"

And then we heard the familiar honk of my Dad's car as he drove into the compound. Oh, the relief! "Daddy's home!" I exulted. "Oh, I'd better go tell him what's happened before the others do."

Ronke was saying something when I bolted out of the room. I should have listened. It would have prepared me for the even bigger surprise that waited for me outside.

My Dad was getting some luggage out from the boot of his car. "Daddy!" I yelled as I approached him. "You can't imagine what just happened."

"Oh, I think you're in for the surprise I got, son," Dad said. And then he stood up, holding up two live chickens, one in each hand. "And we get to prepare it together too."

I had hoped it couldn't get worse. It was too much to hope for.

Oh well, that would not be the last Christmas chicken I would prepare. And like Ronke said, the legend of the Mighty Dayo and the Christmas Chicken still lives on, recounted every Christmas or whenever the family is gathered. It's more hilarious than embarrassing, really. But what can I say? Some family traditions will just never die.

<u>*We are all Equal by Funom Theophilus Makama*</u>

Iniobong happily walks along the street towards the venue of the birthday party, about half a mile from her home. It has been a while she was this excited and she couldn't wait to join in the mood of celebrations and happiness.

She is wearing a pink dress designed in flowery embroidery across its length on the right side. The short sleeve dress is a new one, bought by her mother for this occasion. She is carrying a gift for the celebrant, Sarah, the smartest girl, not only in her class but in the entire set.

Right from the moment the birthday party was announced in class, Iniobong had fantasized and dreamt of this occasion, not once or twice, but several times. She gets to the gate and can hear the loud music that is superimposed with children's voices and disorderliness. She knocks on the gate.

A girl of her age but a bit taller and slimmer comes out. "Ini, what are you doing here?"
Iniobong is surprised. "How do you mean? It is your birthday."

Sarah looks at her with an insulting stare and laughs sarcastically. "Yes, it is my birthday and so? Were you invited? Did I personally ask you to come?"

Iniobong is yet to recover from her shock. "I do not understand. Teacher Evelyn announced it in class on Friday and specifically said that everyone is invited. Should I still expect a personal invitation from you?"

Sarah laughs out loud whilst looking away, into the compound as she calls out. "Ndifreke, Ekaette, please come, come, come oh. Come and see something."

Two of Sarah's friends rush to the scene and instantly join in making fun of Iniobong, but she pleads. "Please do not embarrass me like this. I am still wondering what I have done to you girls that makes you treat me this way. I am not as intelligent, not from a family as wealthy, so why are you doing this to me?"

Sarah responds immediately. "Exactly! That is the point, you are trying your best to belong where you don't. I have rejected you from joining our clique, but you will always prove stubborn."

Iniobong objects. "Is this your birthday party only for your clique of friends?"

Ekaette, one of Sarah's friends' shouts: "My friend, what part of 'we are not interested don't you understand'? Leave us alone!"

Ekaette's loud voice draws the attention of the celebrant's mother. She approaches the gate to find out what is happening. "Sarah, what is going on there? Why are you three standing at the gate?"

The three girls smile mischievously as they close the gate and face Sarah's mother. "Nothing ma, we were just making girlish observations." The three reply simultaneously. She ignores their antics, pushing them aside to open the gate, and to her surprise, she meets young Iniobong in a standstill, shedding tears.

Sarah's mother reaches out. "Oh dear! What is the problem? Why are you crying? Why are you even outside in the first place?"

Iniobong responds. "Sarah and her friends hate me so much. They do not like me at all."

Sarah's mother embraces her. "No, I do not think so, how can anyone hate an angel like you? Just look at you, how pretty and innocent you are. Please come in."

Iniobong is relieved. "Thank you very much ma, please accept this gift from me, since Sarah would not accept it." Iniobong hands over the red and white teddy bear she brought for the celebrant to her mother.

"Oh dear, this is lovely. I love it so much and trust me, your friend will love it too. It may not be now, but I promise you that she will." Sarah's mother takes her to the place of the party and hands her over to one of the teachers available to look after her.

The next Wednesday in school, Sarah and her friends constantly stare at Iniobong in contempt. Other pupils rallied around Sarah, from time to time, to either congratulate her or give her the typical attention any queen of their peers attracts.

Iniobong has tried right from year 3 to associate with her and now that they were in year 5, the story is still the same. Sarah and her friends have shown to be of a better class than she is. Iniobong had always felt inferior and needed the validation of belonging in the company of Sarah and her friends.

Just a month ago, when everyone was stating what they wanted to become in the future, Sarah said she wants to be a Medical Doctor, Ekaette a Lawyer, Ndifreke loves mathematics and hopes to be an Engineer. To their amusement, Iniobong said she hopes to be a writer and Lecturer and this aspiration of hers was added to their Arsenal of insults.

Wednesdays are particularly for Physical Education (P.E) classes compulsorily done under the primary school curriculum of Nigeria. During P.E, Iniobong played clapping games with other children while constantly spying on Sarah and her friends.

After about 30 minutes of trying so hard to ignore them, she found the courage to approach them. "Sarah, please forgive me for any wrong I did to you."

Sarah and her friends ignore Iniobong and change the location of their exercise. She follows them to seek their acceptance, but they continue resisting, yelling at her in the process. Iniobong gives up and joins another group to play with. The next day, Sarah returns her teddy bear to her amazement. Iniobong goes to the back of the class and there, she weeps bitterly.

It is exactly 2 days to the end of term and a week to Christmas, Iniobong and her Mum are in the hairdressing saloon preparing for Christmas. While drying her hair, her Mum sits to watch the TV. Twenty-five minutes into dressing her hair, Sarah and her mother enter the same saloon.

Sarah's mother quickly identifies Iniobong and goes to greet them, to Sarah's disapproval. Sarah grudgingly associates herself with them, but her Mum's persistence overshadows her rudeness. The two mothers sit in the waiting area as they have a good time, chatting, laughing, and clapping hands whilst the girls act as if the other isn't in the room. An hour later, Iniobong and her mother leave the saloon. The mothers exchange lovely goodbyes, but their daughters are not gracious to each other at all.

It is the final day of the academic term and report cards are shared. As expected, Sarah tops her class and wins six awards for academic excellence. She flaunts her achievement around, whilst her friends followed her like flies. Iniobong completely minds her business, not giving them the attention, they need, but this doesn't sit well with Sarah.

Sarah and her friends do everything possible to get her attention but to no avail. The girls wander outside the class and return inside, exaggerating their body gestures around other children, all to get Iniobong's attention but she cares less.

This disturbs Sarah and after getting some advice from her friends, she finally approaches Iniobong. "How are you Ini?"

Iniobong opens her eyes in surprise. "Are you talking to me?"

"Yes, I am, Ini. Or don't you want to talk to me?"

Sure, I would love to, but I can't remember any time you ever approached me just to talk."

Sarah smiles. "I am doing it now, aren't we at least age-mates?"

Iniobong refuses to believe what is going on. "Yes, you always say that you are some months older than I am and that I should never think we will be friends."

Sarah comes even closer. "I am so sorry, we are both eight years old, that is all that matters."

Iniobong looks at her suspiciously. "Are you sure you are not up to something?

As you can see, I have been minding my business today."

"Yeah, I noticed that."

"Aha! And you could not take it, right?"

Sarah feigns annoyance. "Why are you so negative about this? I am trying my best to reconcile with you, and you are busy giving me attitude?"

Iniobong smiles but still stands her ground. "If you miss being congratulated, then I congratulate you for doing what you do best. Congratulations, best in Math, English, Social studies, and Neatest girl as well. I am truly happy for you."

Sarah smiles in appreciation and embraces Iniobong, who stands still in shock without reciprocating the gesture. She then withdraws from her body and says: "Come to the play garden by the yellow swing. I and my friends will be waiting for you there."

At this point, Iniobong begins feeling comfortable with her. "What for?"
"We want you to be a part of those that will plan my success party. I also want you to be among my clique during the Christmas period."
Iniobong jumps "Wow! Yes, yes, yes, I will do anything to hang out with you girls." She embraces Sarah in reflex and assures her of her presence.

The two girls leave to the play garden and to exactly where the yellow swing is, which is at a corner that sometimes seems an isolated place. Ekaette, Ndifreke and another girl are waiting and their welcoming gestures as soon as they see their friend and Iniobong kill any fear of the unknown.

When the five girls are together, the four friends form a square, pushing Iniobong to the centre. They begin unleashing a series of insults and mockery and anytime she tries leaving, she is pushed by the girl that is on her way. She turns to different directions to attempt leaving but the same outcome ensures.

Iniobong gives up and remains in one position to accept her fate, receiving all the insults rained at her. The girls notice her resolve and change their strategy to an even more provocative one. Ndifreke brings down her bag from her back and brings out a one-litre fruit juice. Ekaette does the same to bring out the local drink made from purple hibiscus, popularly called *Zobo* drink and Sarah brings out a one-Litre container, full of Ice cream.

They open their drinks and at the same time pour the content on her body. They empty every bottle on her and while she is still relishing in the shock of what just happened, Sarah, holding her already melting ice cream as the bottom of its container rests on her flat widespread palm, smashed it on Iniobong's face.

The container gradually falls off, leaving her face heavily soiled with semi-solid white matter that continuously melts away. She falls on her knees, weeping bitterly. The assault is not over yet. The extra girl brings out a bottle of water and turns the content on the poor kneeling girl. The girls laugh out loud and leave the scene.

Iniobong's father arrives at the school vicinity to pick her up. He searches around but cannot find her. He reports the case to one of the teachers who helps him go around the school. They reach the playground and just when they get to the corner of the yellow swing, Iniobong is seen lying sideways, on her right side with both of her legs flexed at the waist and knee joints, and her wet face on both hands whilst she weeps.

Her body and the ground surrounding her are wet and coloured in different shades of blue and yellow. Her father becomes furious, he lifts her to his shoulders and carries her away. He goes to the principal's office alongside the teacher, and she narrates what happened while being wrapped in a blanket. He takes her away as soon as she started shivering but reassures the school of drastic actions if nothing is done to the perpetrators of the act.

***

It's Christmas and everyone is in high spirits. Iniobong and her two elder brothers who returned from boarding secondary school to spend the holiday with family have been catching up. The two parents are also present, food is already served, and their loud music contributes to the disorderly environmental noise around the vicinity. Then comes a knock on the door and when asked to come in, Sarah and her mother come inside the house to meet an unpleasant mood that only started existing when they showed up.

Sarah's mother speaks. "Your faces have said it all. Good morning mama Ini, papa Ini, good morning. Merry Christmas."

Iniobong's parents reply reluctantly as she continues. "We should have been here earlier, but her stubbornness is what has stopped us. I and her Dad had to be more intentional and drastic before she agreed to come with me. I do not know what to say other than to say sorry. We are very sorry for what happened." Iniobong is in the kitchen, not knowing what is going on.

Her father responds as he faces Sarah. "You seem to be the first and only child, right?"

Sarah stands still, looking downwards and not responding to him, her Mum quickly taps her on the shoulder. "Yes sir." She answers faintly.

Iniobong's father ignores her attitude and continues. "Look around you, Ini has two elder brothers; brothers that can ambush you and treat you the same way you treated their sister. Ini has more protection than you do, irrespective of who you think your parents are. So, count yourself lucky that things are still normal with you."

Iniobong's mother adds. "You completely killed her self-confidence. I have been working on my daughter's confidence all these years and I see great improvement, just for you to shatter it. The last 5 days haven't been easy for all of us because of what we had to pass through to redeem her pride. Sarah, you have not done well at all."

Sarah's mother kneels to the ground and drags her to do the same. "Mama Ini, Papa Ini, we are sorry. We are so sorry for this. I never had the slightest idea that my daughter could do such a thing. She is intelligent, smart and we as parents have been doing our part to see that she is responsible too. I never knew she can go to this extent to harm another."

Iniobong enters the living room and laughs. "Is that Sarah on her knees? I cannot believe it." Sarah looks at her in disdain but Iniobong cares less as she continues. "See Sarah, I have forgiven you. You were expelled from school and asked never to come back, but it was I and my Mum who pleaded on your behalf. Your prizes will be stripped from you and that will be announced in our first assembly next term, I think that is a worthy punishment for you."

Sarah's mother answers in humility. "Thank you, my child, thank you so much for doing that for us. That school is the best around here, I cannot imagine my daughter going to another."

Iniobong walks to Sarah's Mum and raises her. She does the same for Sarah. "You are very smart Sarah. You are intelligent, beautiful, very neat and organized. I adored you. You were my role model and I wanted everything with you, but you treated me less than a human. I have forgiven you but will have nothing to do with you.

You once told me, your Daddy and Mummy have a mansion, so I am not your class. Well, by tomorrow, I will be travelling to Canada to spend the rest of the holiday with my Aunty." Sarah looks at her in surprise as she continues.

"We cannot have it all, but I will never use whatever luxury I enjoy to look down on another person. Do you see all those items just outside the house? My brothers and I will be taking them to the Orphanage and that is where we will be spending the evening of our Christmas- with the fatherless and motherless. Nothing gives joy more than this."

Iniobong's father smiles. "You should expect a different Ini by next term. And as you can see, you have lost an admirer and a fan forever. Think about it Sarah, you had an opportunity for greatness and you blew it away. Next time, when you are in a position of influence, instead of resorting to bullying and intimidation, do your best to be a good example. You are a bright kid. You will be fine."

Sarah becomes remorseful and starts to shed tears. Her mother comforts her and pleads with her to be a good girl. Sarah pleads with Iniobong to join them to go to the Orphanage and despite her refusal, Sarah persists until she agrees.

Now in the Orphanage home, the four children: Iniobong, her two brothers and Sarah, go round, sharing the items they brought for the children. It is a small home consisting of 55 children between the ages of 1 to 9.

There are five care workers present as well, all singing songs of gratitude and the season as they collect the items. Food, clothing, toys, stationaries, and other items are distributed. The joy the children show is so overwhelming that from time to time, Sarah shed a tear. Iniobong gathers the children to recite a poem for them. "I title it, 'Love Opens Doors', I hope you enjoy it."

> *Heaven sits above the sky*
> *Its lasting peace never lies*
> *A gift always in standby*
> *From my Daddy, the good guy.*
> *We can hold hands and go high*
> *One with no legs should not die*
> *And good looks without an eye.*
> *It's Christmas, I should ask why*

Does this love make me cry?
To all, the blessing applies
Bigotry, I'll never try
Because Orphans also fly.
[The children jump in joy]
The night harmattan may buy
The warmth from the sun that says hi
On our hearts for love to ply.
It's Christmas, no one says bye
It's Christmas, you're mine, mine, mine
It's Christmas, bias, we defy
It's Christmas, let goodness pry.

Everyone gives a standing ovation, two of the care workers even shed tears as they appreciate the kind gesture from Iniobong. Sarah is touched and she rushes outside. After a short while, Iniobong follows, to check on her. She meets her at a corner, crying. "Stop crying Sarah, everything is fine."

Sarah objects. "No, nothing is fine Ini, I am a bad girl, a very bad girl. I am so sorry for everything I have done to you, Ini. I feel so ashamed of myself. You are a good girl and I am happy I came here with you."

Iniobong embraces her. "You are a good girl too."

Sarah re-emphasizes. "No, Ini, you are in fact the role model here. I will be glad to be your friend.

Iniobong replies. "We will see…. We will see." Both girls get back inside and join in the mood of the season with the happy orphans.

Christmases of Fondly Fears

by Leke Amoo

My strongest memory of Christmas is that of fear- at least at the beginning of the Christmas season. The very first announcement that informs us that Christmas is near are some loud noises. Hearing these noises from a distance isn't much of a bother at first, in fact, I admit, many times I had been part of those lousy children who contributed to the noises.

But as I grew older the noises became louder and the tubes producing them became more sophisticated. It became clear to me that a weapon was being fashioned out of these enchanting children's toys.

Soon, some adults joined in the noisemaking and even hurt innocent people with these toys. It was at this point that the joy I had for Christmas was replaced with fear.

When the Nigerian government finally placed a ban on rockets, firecrackers, and knockouts, I breathed a sigh of relief. But I must say, Christmas then became sort of boring. I mean, what was Christmas without 'bangers' as we called them?

The feeling of fear that loomed around me and my friends was a necessary part of the fun. But little did I know that a worse fear was growing in my home.

I was 10 years old when we last had a Christmas worth celebrating, then Dad ran into huge debt. And since he had no way to pay, he ran away, leaving us without any warning.

Imagine hearing a knock on your door a few days to Christmas, you open with a smile expecting to see a familiar face. Instead, you're greeted by the face of a peeved stranger. If the stranger is male, he is likely a barber who could cut your ears off or a commercial driver who could run his tyres over your knees. If it's a female, she could be a prostitute that wouldn't mind enslaving Dad's daughters until every dime is paid.

Those were the sort of threats we got.
Creditors came and carted away with anything they could lay their hands on, including my sisters. Thank God for hefty neighbours who fought to free us.

In effect, rather than entertain guests and cook meals, we found ourselves grovelling to merciless people and cooking for others who didn't care about us at all. Creditors filled our house in the daytime and left when it was dark.

For the first time in my life, I looked forward to night times and prayed the day never dawned.

Every day, I stared out the window, watching children on our street having fun with no care or concern in this world and I envied them – these were children who once envied me that my parents are rich or should I say *'were'* rich.

By the next Christmas, Dad was not yet back and there was no way to contact him. There were no phones and no way to track his whereabouts. All we heard was that he was moving from one prayer house to another.

Since it was clear that he wouldn't be back soon, we knew it was best for everyone's sanity that we desert the house. So, for three years, we stayed away from home during Christmas and the New Year celebrations.
It was during one of such escape seasons that I was wrongly accused of a crime and locked up in a police cell for 10 days. I was barely 13 years old and this happened during Easter. So, you can say I ran away from Christmas trouble but landed in a worse condition on Easter. No persecution could be worse!

After my 14th birthday, Dad finally returned home.

He promised to right his wrongs and assured us that things would be better thenceforth. He had met with God on his trip and was encouraged to go back home, pick up his former business that failed and that he would excel at it.

Things started turning around for good. I was 17 years old when he fulfilled his promise to make it up to us. He killed a goat for Christmas, gave us money to cook rice and we bought lots of chicken.

To me, that moment was more than a celebration of the birth of Jesus but also a celebration of the death of fear – fear that anyone could ever steal the joy of Christmas from me and my family.

New Shoes For Christmas
by Adebola Adisa

I always looked forward to *Decoration Day*.

It was our unwritten family tradition.

We always decorated our massive white Christmas tree after lunch on the last Sunday of every November.

However, it did not look like we would be decorating this year.

Nothing seemed to be the same this year, and it was already 20 days to Christmas.

Mummy had not done any Christmas food shopping, nor were the red, green, silver and gold decorations or the Christmas tree in sight. There was no advent chocolate calendar for the Christmas day countdown, and I had not yet caught sight of my new shoes either.

Dad always brought the tree, shiny bubbles, ribbons, and other decorations out of our garage on the Saturday evening, before our Decoration Day.

As far as I knew, we had never missed this tradition.

Our family had so many traditions, but the Christmas one was the ultimate and rightly so. The Christmas season always brought out kindness, even from the hard-hearted.

Was it not during the last Christmas that my uncle, David, let me get away with entering his room to admire his new customised Chelsea football T-shirt? Everyone knew that my uncle's room was a no-go area, but my curiosity made me forget this. Anyway, he was not cross with me and let me off that one time.

However, this Christmas, I knew that something was not quite right, but I could not put a finger on what it was.

Our large bright, warm, busy, and bubbly house no longer felt the same. It felt very dark, cold, lonely, and quiet.

Mummy was no longer kind to me, she seldom spoke, and anytime she did, she would either shout or snap at me impatiently.

She seemed upset all the time, and I had seen her crying a few times, but each time, she tried to hide her tears by quickly cleaning them away with the back of her arm.

Their bedroom was always locked and appeared dark whenever I peeped through the keyhole.

Mummy no longer sat on her favourite pink coloured chair in her favourite room in the house, her study.

When the COVID-19 pandemic began, she converted her study to a home office, so that she could work from home.

Whenever I returned from school, she always allowed me to sit quietly, whilst I watched her work.

She always appeared excited, happy and spoke nicely to the people she called her clients.

Then gradually, it all changed, and she began to stay for longer periods all alone in their bedroom, she stopped allowing me to come into her home office, and after a while, she stopped working from home.

She also stopped watching TV or eating dinner with us at the dining table.

After a while, Mummy never seemed to leave their bedroom and only our family Doctor, Dr Eni went in there. She came to see Mummy every Saturday morning and was in the room for long periods before leaving.

I liked Dr Eni, who always looked smart in her long white coat, often with a black stethoscope hanging around her neck. She smiled a lot and was always kind to me, and brought little treats like Kit Kat chocolate and Haribo sweets each time she visited. Whenever I asked if Mummy was alright, she nodded and said;

Your Mummy will be fine

That did not feel reassuring though, because I knew that doctors often saw people when they were ill, which meant that Mummy was sick. I hated going to the hospital to see Dr Eni anytime I had a fever or pain somewhere, though the medicines always made me feel better.

I never saw Daddy. He was never there when I woke up in the morning and probably came back home well past my bedtime. Uncle David did everything for me now since Mummy was no longer interested in doing anything.

He made my breakfast, lunch, and dinner, made sure I was ready for school and drove me to school. He told me that I had to stay at the after-school club and picked me up late in the afternoon. I enjoyed being at after school club because my best friend Bee Bee attended too. The weekends were awful as no one seemed to care what I did, and I had to come up with my ideas to keep the boredom away.

Why didn't Mummy and Daddy care about me anymore?

It was already mid-December, yet I had not caught sight of my Christmas shoes. Dad always bought my shoes by the first day of December and kept them in the top cupboard of the wardrobe in their bedroom, and we all pretended that it was not there.

Then every evening in December, after Dad returned from work, I would sing and dance with Mummy and Daddy cheering me on.

Christmas is coming
Daddy buy shoes for me o o
Christmas is coming
Daddy buy shoes for me o o
New shoes for me o o
New shoes for me o o

Mummy and Daddy always found it funny.
However, nothing seemed to be happening this year.
There was no one to watch me sing and dance.
The thought crossed my mind to ask my uncle David to watch me sing and dance
But it was no use because he always seemed tired or busy doing the household chores.
Uncle David told me that our house help Mary had left without any reason.

Everyone had to be careful because of the COVID-19 pandemic, so there were no face-to-face birthday parties or playdates.
Remote zoom parties were all we had, even though it was something, it was not quite the same.

It felt like I was all on my own, and no one seemed to care!

Then I remembered that Mummy always told me that we were not on our own.

She always said that God is watching us, even when we feel lonely and when we are sleeping or ill.

She always said that we could talk to him, and he hears us.

So, I decided to write a letter to God.

Dear God,

My Mummy said that you are always watching us. She also said that you are always with us when we feel lost and lonely. She said that you can make things better whenever they do not feel right.

God, would you please make things better in our house?

Please let my Mummy come out of her dark room and be happy again, she always seems sad, not wishing to speak to any of us in the house.

Make my Daddy come into my room to kiss me goodbye whenever he leaves the house in the morning.

Let my Daddy come back home early so, that I can sing the Daddy buy shoes for me song.

Let Mummy and Daddy be happy to watch me dance the new floss dance style I just learnt on YouTube.

God, would you help our uncle David so that he doesn't get too tired or busy. Maybe my Granny could come for a visit once the lockdown is over.

That would be very nice, dear God.

Can you remind Mummy and Daddy to come and watch our Nativity at school?

You know that I am playing the role of Joseph, the father of Jesus.

Finally, let us have Decoration Day and a lovely Christmas.

Thank you and amen.

It's me.

Moyo xx

PS

Can you remind Daddy to buy my Christmas shoes?

I was quite happy with my letter to God, so I put it in a white envelope and kept it on our large, brown dining table.

I hoped that God would find it there since Mummy had told me that God is everywhere.

That night, I slept a little bit better.

Uncle David was super nice too and read a bit from my favourite night-time book when I asked him to.
The next morning, I rushed to the dining room to check if God had picked up my letter.
He had not!

That made me feel very sad, and I did not want to eat my breakfast. But Uncle David insisted because I would be hungry at school if I did not, so I ate most of my cornflakes.
The letter was all that I could think about at school, and I got into trouble with our class teacher, Miss Peppy, a few times for not listening in class.
After school, she called me to her desk and asked me what was wrong.
I explained everything and told her that I was upset that God did not read my letter. She told me that I should just be patient, that He would.
After many days, the letter was exactly where I left it, and I soon gave up on God ever reading it.

Then, it happened.
One day, after returning from swimming lessons at the community centre, I noticed that the letter was gone.

I was ecstatic. Miss Peggy was right after all. Even though Mummy and Daddy were not there, I started singing my song and dancing the floss dance.

Christmas is coming
Daddy buy shoes for me o o
Christmas is coming
Daddy buy shoes for me o o
New shoes for me o o
New shoes for me o o

I slept well that night.
When I returned from school the next day, I was pleasantly surprised to see Mummy sitting in the living room watching a Nollywood movie on Netflix. She smiled, and I ran to hug her asking if I could watch the movie with her. I was over the moon when she said that I could.

The title of the movie was "The Wedding Party." It was hilarious and full of good cheer and lots of joyous music to dance to.
I wanted to teach Mummy how to do the floss dance, however, she said she was too tired but was happy to watch me dance. Then we went to the dining room together and ate Indomie

noodles and boiled egg which Uncle David made for lunch.

After lunch, Mummy said she needed to sleep, but she allowed me to walk with her into her room. I was so happy that my Mummy was no longer sad.

I tried to wait up for Daddy to come home, but when he was yet to return by 8:00 pm, Uncle David said that I needed to go to bed.

I remembered how Mummy always said.

Early to bed,
Early to rise and shine

From then on, Mummy always seemed to be waiting for me to return home from school, and we continued to watch Nollywood movies every day. She was gradually getting back to her old self.

She was smiling more and even allowed me to fall asleep in her bed during my siesta time.

Her room was no longer dark because she now kept the curtains pulled back, which let in the bright shining sunlight.

One day, I told Mummy about our Nativity at school and asked her if she and Daddy would come. She said she didn't think she could, and

Daddy was probably too busy. She said my Uncle David would be coming though. I knew that she had not left the house for a very long time and though I was sad, I left it at that.

Soon, Daddy began coming home early, and we started having dinner together again, just like old times.
I was so happy again.
We were all happy again.
From then on, at bedtime, Daddy always read a bedtime story to me and kissed me goodnight.
At times he and Mummy both read to me.
Things were getting back to normal again, but we still didn't have our Christmas tree up, and Daddy had not bought my Christmas shoes.

I woke up quite excited because that day was *Nativity Day*!
The headteacher said that since the lockdown was over, we didn't need to show the Nativity play to our friends and family on zoom anymore, that everyone could attend if they maintained social distance and wore their masks.

I was a little sad that only uncle David was coming to watch me at school, but that was still better than if no one was coming.

Bee Bee told me that his parents were away in America, and no one was coming to see him act in his role as the Nativity donkey.

I told him that my uncle David would watch both of us act in our school Nativity and would get us ice cream and popcorn from the tuck shop after, and that made him happy.

Once we were all dressed in our costumes, Miss Peggy told us all to do our best and smile a lot, and we all promised to.

As soon as I stepped onto the podium with Mary and the donkey pretending to be on our way to Bethlehem, right there at the front was my Uncle David, and next to him was Mummy, Daddy, and Granny.

What a lovely surprise!

I was about to jump down from the podium to give them a tight hug but stopped myself from doing that when I saw Miss Peggy signal to me to behave.

I don't quite know how I managed to stay focused because I was beside myself and full of so much joy.

Our Nativity could not end soon enough.

Our performance was brilliant, and everyone clapped for us.

Once we could, I ran straight to where everyone was and hugged them.

I could not quite believe it.

God did what I asked for and more.

When we got home, I was in for yet another surprise!

Our white Christmas tree was up in the living room, but without the red, green, silver and gold bubbles, ribbons, and other decorations. Those were all in a large brown cardboard box by the side of the tree.

Daddy said that we could all decorate it together, so we did.

Granny brought out all the special goodies that she always brought for me, and not even one was missing. There were spicy prawns, fried plantain, fried bean cakes, and a knitted blue and white PJ masks sweater.

I gave Granny the warmest hug ever and said *thank you* several times over.

Uncle David seemed the happiest of all because Granny told him that she was taking over the kitchen that day, and he seemed relieved.

I asked everyone if they would watch me sing and dance, and they said okay.

So, I sang my "Daddy buy shoes for me" song, and Mummy and I danced the floss.

Christmas is coming
Daddy buy shoes for me o o
Christmas is coming
Daddy buy shoes for me o o
New shoes for me o o
New shoes for me o o

I even taught Daddy how to do the floss dance, but he could not do it correctly. Granny said that Daddy had always been a poor dancer, and we all laughed at him.

At bedtime, Daddy carried me to my room, and he and Mummy asked me if I knew why things had been very different at home for the last few months.

I said that I didn't know.

Mummy explained that she had felt very sad for a long time, did not feel well before, and could not manage or cope with the stress at work or getting things done at home all at the same time. She said that the lockdown had made things worse because she could not meet up with her friends or other close family members either.

She needed a lot of help, such as talking to someone who helped her understand what she was going through, and was also taking medicines prescribed by Dr Eni.

She felt better now but still needed to take things easy for a bit.

Mummy said she was sorry for when she snapped at me and for not being fun to be around in the past.

Daddy said he had needed to work harder so that we could still afford all the lovely things that we were all used to, especially with Mummy not being able to work just then.

However, he had learnt that the best thing in life is his family and now knew the importance of being present for the family.

He said that money wasn't everything.

He and Mummy had spoken to people who helped them understand things better.

He felt sorry about everything and hoped that we would be the lovely, happy family that we had been before.

Then they both said that I could ask them any question at any time.

I said it was all okay. I was not sure about all that they said, but all I knew was that I was sad before. Now I was back to being happy because everyone was smiling again.

Then Daddy and Mummy read to me from *Dr Facts Continents of the World* storybook.

I must have nodded off to sleep.

The next morning Daddy came into my room and told me that he wanted to show me something.

He took me to their bedroom, and Mummy, who was sitting at the edge of the bed, was grinning.

Daddy pointed to the large black box sitting at the top of the open wardrobe.

I already knew what it was and jumped up and down in excitement.

Before I could say anything, he reached out and brought out the black box, which he gave to me.

I opened it immediately and in there were my special shoes, my Sketchers trainers.

It was exactly what I dreamed of!

I was speechless!

I was so happy!

Then I said *thank you* to Daddy and Mummy and gave them both a tight hug.

As I rushed off to tell my Uncle David, I remembered that everything had happened just like I had asked.

I knew that I had to say a special prayer to thank God for reading my letter, and for doing everything that I asked for!

Another Christmas Story

by Niyi Marcus

"Can you read me another story, Mum?" Jide asked, his eyes wide awake, brimming with excitement.

It was now 10 pm and Ronke was thinking about the quickest way she could get Jide to sleep. Bedtime stories were not working this time, and she had to get up early in the morning to prepare the Christmas feast.

She could hear the crackling of the fat goose grandpa had sent in the previous day. She thought about the delicious roast goose meat she will prepare, the seasoning already set on the kitchen counter.

"Another story, Mum!" Jide pleaded. This time, he was tugging at Ronke's sleeves and flapping his feet against the bedrails. It was his eighth birthday tomorrow and he was having a big party. Everyone was going to be there. The neighbours' kids, the Smiths from church, the elderly lady that lives down the road who always gave him cookies.

He could smell the aroma of food wafting across from the pantry. The living room was also well set with the decorations Dad had hung up earlier in the day. The year before, he got a beautiful blue bicycle as his birthday present. He wondered what this year's gift would be.

Jide always looked forward to his birthday party every year which he celebrates on Christmas Day. There was so much to eat and drink. He loved the Christmas decorations hanging all around the house, and the rooms bursting full of people, coming in and out. He enjoyed singing Jingle Bells with his friends while racing around the house with a lit candle.

The part he looked forward to the most was getting a huge chunk of his birthday cake. He had caught a glimpse of the cake sitting majestically on top of the dining table. It was a huge blue cake decorated with cream-coloured icing and garnished with chocolate toppings.

After the third story, Ronke was sure he had fallen asleep now. She tucked Jide into bed, kissed him goodnight and flicked off the lamp on the bedside table. She sighed and smiled, satisfied at how much she had been able to accomplish for the day, and prepared to go to bed. She had a long day ahead of her tomorrow. Little did she know that Jide had a plan of his own.

Jide listened as the sounds of footsteps ascending the staircase leading to the bedroom upstairs faded off in the distance, and then he waited for a few more minutes just to be sure. Whisking off the bedsheet, he gently tiptoed to the hallway with bated breath. Finally, he was at the entrance to the dining room. He held his breath, turned the doorknob ever so stealthily, and gently pushed the door open.

His heart missed a beat when the door came open with a loud sharp shrill. Jide stopped in his tracks, worried that he had blown his cover. He listened intently for his Dad's voice, and his Mum's footsteps, but there was only a deafening silence and pitch blackness. A smile lit his face as the aroma of the cake filled his nostrils, and he began to salivate. He was going to eat a mighty piece tomorrow, all by himself.

Illuminated by the lights from the big Christmas tree decorations, Jide could see his wrapped birthday present set on the table. The wrapping paper had the green design of a football pitch, which left him more curious as to what it could be. He moved closer to the table to have a better look and then he suddenly fell with a loud crashing sound. He had tripped on something and knocked his head against the dining table.

As Jide winced with pain in the dark, he could immediately feel his face covered in something soft and sticky. He heard heavy footsteps racing down the staircase, and down the hallway. In a few seconds, lights flooded the room to reveal what he had done. He was lying on the floor beside the dining table, his birthday cake toppled over beside him!

Ronke's mouth was agape in utter disbelief. His Dad, Kunle also flew into the room, his arms akimbo, and his eyes filled with questions. The silence was punctuated by a loud wail from Jide, who now realised what he had done. His beautiful birthday cake had now fallen apart, smeared across his face and pyjamas. Ronke helped him off the floor and wiped some of the cake off his face with a wet cloth.

"I- I- I- did- not- not- mean- mean- to… It was a mi- mi- mis-take…" Jide's words bobbed in between his sobs.
"And there goes your beautiful birthday cake. Anyway, that should not be a problem. We can celebrate without a birthday cake." Kunle said.

"What's a birthday without a birthday cake?", replied Ronke.
"Well, I did not have a birthday cake to celebrate my birthdays when I was growing up. So, a cake is really a luxury", Kunle teased.

"Oh, come on, Kunle!", Ronke retorted. "He already feels terrible, and you can see that".
The tears continue to fall from Jide's face. He thought about all his friends who would be coming for this birthday. There would be no cake-cutting this year.

"I am sorry, Mum and Dad, I just wanted to see what you had gotten me for my birthday," Jide said, wiping his eyes with the back of his hand. "Come on, Jide," Kunle continued. "You have the most beautiful birthday present every year. Don't you know your birthday comes at the best time of the year? Who else is as lucky to be born on Christmas day?"
The rattling sounds of fireworks continued to fill the air, mixed with the melodious humming of a Christmas chorus from the chapel across the road.

"I have an idea!" Ronke said, her eyes brightening.
"Come with me," she continued, pulling Jide as they ran along past the corridor to the front porch of the house.

"Now, look at that!" Ronke said, pointing towards the sky.

Jide instantly forgot about his crumbled cake, marvelling at the most stunning sight he had ever seen. The sky was beautifully lit with fireworks, yellow, gold, and red lights littering the dark blue horizon, sparkling among the uncountable glimmering stars. Just then, another firework exploded with a loud bang, and a big bright MERRY CHRISTMAS formed in the sky.

Jide thought to himself, Dad was right. What a treat it was to see these colourful firework displays every year. Certainly, this was the perfect birthday gift; he felt like the luckiest boy in the world!

Banwo's Conquest And The Christmas Bells

by Kayode .O. Sinmidele Valentine

"Halt!"
"Left – left, left – left! Left – right; left – right;
Left – right; halt."

"Left – right; left – right; left – right, forwarrrrrrd march! One, two, three, four!"
"Halt!"
"And what in heavens' name do you think you are doing, David?"

The District Chief yelled for the umpteenth time today.
"Will you please step aside?" He blurted out!

David sluggishly lost the rhythm as his other colleagues fanned out with precision, in the three equidistant directions as earlier marked out. He wished he didn't have to come to work today. David had frantically made further efforts to stay focused in this morning parade but the mental fog he was experiencing wouldn't give him a chance.

Worse still, the district chief came to lead today's parade voicing his orders with so much temerity; the forthcoming National Heroes' Day must not suffer ridicule. But today, David was being side-lined.
Standing about 50 metres away from the parade ground, he wiped the tears that had begun to drip down as he remembered 'Banwo's critical state. A young teenager

battling for his life in a dramatic event that shocked everyone including his teachers and schoolmates. How his son - 'Banwo became a shadow of himself had left his father David more disoriented.

Last night was tough; nights are usually the toughest times for them as young 'Banwo battled poor sleep – insomnia from his chronic illness. Despite having all his medications, the sick lad still relapsed like a drowning, helpless, and naïve swimmer.

"David! What on earth is wrong with you?"

"Why were you not paying attention to your instructions even with the district chief in the lead?"

Captain Solanke was fuming.

"Well, I have been asked to hand you a suspension for 4 weeks to serve as a deterrent unto others." Solanke continued.

"You were nearly expelled if not that I was profusely apologizing on your behalf."

He thanked his immediate boss as he packed a few needed items from the little table in his office; returning the keys to the janitor, David left the Fire service centre, Ikeja with such a heavy heart.

As he approached their "new home", his heart became heavier. He was contemplating what he would tell his wife about his refusal to yield to her unsolicited advice. His wife had pleaded with him not to bother going to work earlier in the day, but he wouldn't listen. Moradeke knew her husband of 16 years very well. The stress of looking after 'Banwo was getting to him, she could feel his subtle aggression.

"You won't pay attention to your parade today and you should call in sick,"
Moradeke had said, dropping the cobweb-entangled long broom she had used to clean the dusty brown ceilings of their newly found accommodation. They could no longer afford the rent of their old house due to the medical bills of their only son – 'Banwo. Mr and Mrs David Banjoko had to move to cheaper accommodation in Akowonjo – a suburb in Lagos. They thought they could manage their lives by saving more from the exorbitant rent they paid at their former high-brow Lekki abode in Lagos Island. But with 'Banwo in and out of the hospital, that was a mirage...

Mrs Chioma Pepple pointed at the girl wearing a fuchsia hair bond around her *Suku*: that central and singly rounded plaited hair like the knob of a door handle.

"You, what is a large area of water surrounded by a land called?"

Bisola looked to the back pretending she was not the only one with such a colourful hair accessory in year 8: Class of 21 boys and 15 girls. Mrs Pepple grinned and took a few steps to the side of the class, stopping suddenly at about 2 desks to Bisola, "Yes, you!"

Bisola forced a smile and looked towards her friend – 'Banwo who was whispering – 'lake', 'lake' in a monotone. Their teacher couldn't see the parabolic message they were exchanging but turned back to her waiting teaching board when Bisola echoed the answer as Lake. Not done, the teacher asked further.

"The examples of the lakes in Africa are?"

Mrs Pepple had now moved further away from the front of the class. She was standing directly in front of 'Banwo, looking straight into Bisola's eyes, both pupils walled off from each other by their intuitive class teacher. Bisola had no answers but looked embarrassed before saying so. Subsequently, Mrs Pepple turned to 'Banwo for a response and the young lad stood up, reeling out:

"Lake Tanganyika – the longest freshwater lake in the world, located majorly between Tanzania and Burundi."

"There is also the Lake Chad – the largest lake in West Africa – located in the far west of Chad and the northeast of Nigeria with some parts extending into Cameroon and Niger."

Although Mrs Pepple hid her excitement for such a bunch of smart answers, the English Language teacher scolded 'Banwo for not allowing his friend to think and be independent. Nevertheless, the class had roared at the peak of their brilliant mate's answers to Mrs Pepple's morning drills.

They knew their experienced female teacher from the city of Port Harcourt loved to quiz them about people and places in their English class every Monday. She had a flair for teaching new words too and they often gawk at her vocabulary – answering few questions only – anytime the hero of the class – 'Banwo missed that English period.

'Banwo is a smart 12-year-old kid. He has been handed double promotions twice in his basic school and his father rejected it on both occasions. Firstly, from year 1 to year 3. His father would have none of those automatic promotions, thus 'Banwo went through year 2 before year 3.

However, at the 2nd offer of double promotion for him from year 4 to year 6, the Father's negative response could not be sustained because it came with a mouth-watering scholarship. The type of scholarship that arm-twisted the father: with expenses covered for those years. If Mr Banjoko had said no to skipping the contentious year 5 class for his son, the scholarship would go to the 2nd best student in year 4. It was Mrs Banjoko that prevailed on her husband to let go so that they could save money for the rainy days thus Banwo completed his year 6 with a scholarship into the high school.

***

Those were the happiest days for the Banjokos. Devastatingly at the high school, the overall good fortune of the family was caught short a few weeks into 'Banwo's 1st term in year 10. The second period was almost over when 'Banwo felt some sudden restlessness; his head ached. He stood up from his desk after taking permission to use the loo, from the Science teacher.

He had barely walked to the door when he collapsed and started twitching. His eyes were rolled upward and the only thing obvious was the white part of the eye – the sclera. His body was stiff, and his limbs moved uncontrollably in the air. Thick saliva had gathered at the right corner of his mouth, oozing and making its way to the bare floor effortlessly. He looked as if was dying with that foaming from his mouth.

His classmates ran away from the class shouting:

"Warapa! Warapa! Warapa!"

Warapa was the word for epilepsy in the local parlance and the belief was you must not step on the spit or you would be infected like catching the deadly Ebola disease. At least, that was what they thought. It took the efforts of both the School VP and Mr Cole – the teacher whose period was rounding off - to carry 'Banwo to the sickbay. He didn't recover from the sudden event until his parents came in to take him away. It was a bad day for the Banjokos.

Unfortunately, it took more than 4 weeks for 'Banwo's recovery while his parents searched for a cure to their son's malady. It was at Eko Island hospital that they got the first diagnosis after series of investigations: Recalcitrant Temporal lobe epilepsy. David was shell-shocked. No one in the family has had such a diagnosis as far he was aware, and Mrs Banjoko went numb.

Epilepsy in his only son seemed far-reaching. To put their young child through a daily drug therapy of many years to come became a nightmare. And realizing that the discontinuation of the drugs could result in repeated seizures - that the doctors could not explain its origin all along - was a terrible disaster.

For the Banjokos', they knew 'Banwo may have to be on the anti-epileptic drugs for the rest of his life. And anytime they witnessed a seizure episode after a few seizure-free days, their hearts sank deeper and confirmed their worst fears: Their son is on a journey of lifelong medication.

Although 'Banwo's doctor (specifically called the neurologist) tried to reassure them, they knew he was just doing his job. What they had read about "stubborn" seizures like their son's was mind-boggling.

Grandpa Banjoko had to come to Lagos to see his grandchild from their village when he heard the distressing news. Grandpa came in the company of his wife – the grandma Banjoko. Their only grandson with a disease unknown in the family lineage made them heartbroken repeatedly, as they witnessed some of the seizures.

Although they went to church quite often, Mr and Mrs Banjoko felt abandoned by all the powers they knew; temporal or divine. Mr David Banjoko could no longer ring the bell for morning prayers and Mrs Banjoko felt despondent.

Sometimes, Mrs Moradeke Banjoko would mumble when her heart begged for more prayers; unable to say any words loudly. For an only child that she waited so long to have, this is a calamity of an unquantifiable emotional let-down. And when the red-light bulb that blinks at their Home Altar, signifying the Sacred Heart of Jesus' enrolment in their abode - went out, Mrs Banjoko did not replace it.

The Madonna image carrying the Baby Jesus no longer inspired her too. No flowers, no light adorning the family altar.

'Banwo, "their light and flowers" had fallen sick, leaving them with many unanswered questions:

"Would he lose tone in the next minute and fall?"

"Would he twitch and bang his head when no one is watching?"

"How did their brilliant son 'catch' epilepsy?"

If Moradeke did not know her son's next episode of those frightening involuntary movements, she knew one thing so sure: Her prayers seemed to be like the proverbial Greek gifts that came with more harm than good.

***

"Don't let him touch you or you will start clenching your teeth…"

Started Ben but 'Banwo didn't let him finish before dropping the popular line to Ben's dismay.

"And then you'd keep soiling your uniform with urine!"

Banwo stood for a while watching the girls and boys as they left one by one. First, it was Damilola who stepped out of the netball court, Siji with Daniel bounced off after. Next was Risquat with Aliyah and then Alex. Bisola – his friend from the basic school left at the last moment. She whispered to 'Banwo some lines so rough and almost un-deciphered:

"Get a life or you're screwed. You could have stayed away, ah!!!

You ruined these afternoon games. You know" 'Banwo stood for a moment, his hands shaking, his face started twitching and then the tears rolled down; it was not another seizure. He knew it. It was his emotions betraying him. Since his return from his compulsory sick leave, he had to struggle for everything.

Firstly, the parents of his classmates were enraged at his resumption and many of them wrote the school management requesting 'Banwo's medical report before he is allowed to join other pupils. Of course, it was his friends who told their parents at home.

After a long battle with the medical report clarifying that Banjoko's seizures are not infectious and so cannot be caught like catching the flu, they allowed him to resume.

Nonetheless, each student moved their chairs and tables away from him.

'Banwo subsequently became the boy by the door. At other times during morning class, he sleeps off, his morning dose of anti-seizure drugs – Tegretol – delivering its sedative effect to his brain.

Factually, the fear of keeping him from seizures that could occur during school hours made his parents reluctant to bring down the dose of his anti-epileptic drugs, when his neurologist proposed this. They don't want to risk a seizure during the class sessions. And truly, 'Banwo does not get fully "clear" from drowsiness until after the short break by 11:00 am; with 2 periods done and dusted at that point, he often looked lost even at the third period.

Sadly, by the end of that term, 'Banwo's scores plummeted significantly, failing 4 of his core subjects namely Mathematics, English, Physics and Biology. Chemistry was the only core subject passed with a B minus. For someone who led the class like a warrior of the land, it was "Banwo's lowest ebb and when his class teacher saw his result, she wept uncontrollably. Her once upon a time trail-blazing student, would be repeating year 10.

The school management also wrote an emotional letter to the Banjokos stating why they think their son should stay off school for a while to recuperate from his present ailment. Mrs Moradeke Banjoko became inconsolable. Her school-loving and scholarship-winning son had been handed a stay home notice.

***

As the new session began, 'Banwo insisted he would resume with the school. He joined the new students in his old class - the year 10 grade and took his classes one after the other. He had learnt to ask for a cup of coffee every morning before leaving home as this prevented him from his disturbing morning somnolence or sleepiness in the class.

The class was more meaningful. His new classmates had heard about the repeaters in their class and they knew 'Banwo was one of them. The three terms flew quickly and 'Banwo's success in the exams was undisputable after clenching the 7th position overall among all his year 10 mates and was duly promoted to the next class - Year 11.

Although his last brain scan was still abnormal and his brain tracing called EEG* were still showing lots of unusual waves, 'Banwo was optimistic he could go on with seizures occurring less during the day. His parents on the other were not.

They knew the meaning of the 'recalcitrant epilepsy' in their child's diagnosis and the persistently poor brain imaging. David and Moradeke Banjoko still avoided morning prayers by staying late in bed.

Nonetheless, 'Banwo's new year 11 class kickstarted with an open invitation from the State educational board. They wanted all the Senior Secondary students (Year 10 - 12) in Lagos state to participate in the biennial State Governor's spelling Bee competition. 'Banwo's school - the Eko international College got the invitation letter also and immediately went into an action plan.
However, the school decided to present only their year 12 pupils and conducted a mock examination to that effect. Ten pupils were

selected for a final knockout session and Mrs Pepple was not surprised to find 'Banwo's name missing from the list. Yet, Mrs Pepple did not agree with the notions flying around in the school:

"Who can guarantee that 'Banwo wouldn't fall and twitch at the podium of fame when questions get to the peak? Well, the school does not need bad publicity in a fierce and keenly-contested competition really."

Expectedly, news reached 'Banwo that some of his former classmates in the Year 12 class had been selected for the state spelling Bee competition and he didn't mention this to his parents. Rather, every morning when no one in the house had woken up, 'Banwo looked to the Family altar in the house and asked no one in particular;

"When will you lighten the burden of shame that I carry every day?

"When will my seizures be gone and my friends will be able to hug me?"

"When will you make my Dad ring the morning bell for prayers again?

He would look on briefly hoping to hear a sign that someone was listening like his parents had taught him before his illness started. Nowadays, his parents have subtly ignored the morning devotions. Except for the ticking of the wall clock, no other sounds would be audible.

Eventually, as the quiz competition drew closer, 5 students from the year 12 class of Eko international College, were listed, having scored the highest scores at the school's mock finals: Shileola, Adetunji, Victor, Amara and Patricia.

In the real sense of it, the Quiz organizers expected the school to have come up to the competition with their students tagged as the semifinalists, having won the school mock rehearsals known as the quarterfinals.

As early as 7:30 am on the day of the competition, the Eko College's school bus was running its engine when the qualified semifinalists hopped into the bus, picking varied spaces in the 18-seater light blue shuttle school bus. The driver was behind the steering while the school Mathematics' teacher took one of the front seats.

Nevertheless, Mrs Pepple needed to finish her first lesson with the Year 11 Class thus she stayed behind hoping to finish early to tag along. The venue of the competition was the National Theatre, Iganmu Lagos – a - 30-minute drive from the school. For a competition scheduled for 9:30 am, 7:45 am was a good time to move. The team could not wait for Mrs Pepple in the long run.

Moreover, the students were very tense for obvious reasons and Mr Soladayo – the teacher accompanying them tried to cheer them up with a few jokes about competitions and ended his chit-chats with "May the best school win"; to which they all chorused – Amen.

The driver announced a change of route because it was the market day at the adjoining popular Apongbon market: 8:00 am. They all sighed; Lagos traffic jams like magic. Adetunji brought out some chocolates from his bag; his aunt had just arrived from Europe and the smell was good. His friends loved the taste too.

The driver was mumbling something about another traffic jam in his new direction: 8:20 am. The google map kept turning, albeit, giving the distance as "the same 15 minutes to the end of the trip" in the last 45 minutes of this tough journey.

"Each school should send in two teachers for the State competition,"
"I thought I made that clear, Mrs Pepple", the 54-year old Principal - Elder Oluojekojutimi added that last line to his displeasure when he met Mrs Pepple still within the school premises when the contestants had left earlier. He walked away mumbling more words to register his dissatisfaction.

Meanwhile, Mrs Pepple had finished her class at 8:40 am, barely 5 minutes before the Principal saw her. She drove swiftly as she listened to the traffic news avoiding Apongbon market and its adjoining routes.

***

The magnificent hall was filled to the brim with different colours of the school uniforms competing for attention too. The echo effects of the large space within the building had been eliminated with padded walls and mounted speakers. When the Quizmaster appeared and started the introduction of schools present, Eko college students had just arrived but could not come in.

Adetunji, Amara, Victor and Shileola were vomiting and had gone to the loo thrice on arrival. By the time they were called, the driver had withdrawn them to the nearest hospital leaving a discombobulated Patricia behind.

Mrs Pepple walked into the busy hall and was shocked not to see the Eko College delegates on the stand. The Quizmaster would not accept Patricia alone, he would only take at least two students from the school for the competition. Eko international college, therefore, stood nullified of the 25 schools present.

Mrs Pepple hurried to the podium and thrust a name into the Quiz master's hand. Patricia Ifemade and 'Banwo Banjoko mounted the stage and stood behind the school's name. Mrs Pepple had asked 'Banwo to come along and have a feel of the day as she rounded off her period at his class - the year 11 class.

The questions flew back and forth at the Spelling BEE Competition till 3 schools were standing for the finals. 'Banwo and Patricia shone brilliantly, beating other 24 schools to be at 2nd position at the Final round. Adetunji and his friends battled food poisoning at the hospital, the chocolates he brought were expired and he took them without telling the Aunt. Patricia had peanut allergies so she passed the chocolates over without tasting them.

Meanwhile, the final General Knowledge question was projected as the fastest finger to win:
"The longest freshwater lake in Africa is?"
The hall went silent.
You could hear if a pin drops within the seconds.
And in a jiffy,
'Banwo pressed the bell and spelt:
"T.A.N.G.A.N.Y.I.K.A" in a breath!
Mrs Pepple with an uncontrollable and beatific smile, ran to the podium swinging the pair of her school winners, one after the other. And although she lifted and swung 'Banwo for a longer time, it was understandable.

Elder Oluojekojutimi and his team were ecstatic, their school won the State Governor's Spell Bee competition for the first time in their

25 years of being established and their 'Banwo was the highest scoring contestant. Plus, that feat qualified 'Banwo as the enviable one-day Governor of the year!

The one–day governor with many privileges for the whole day. And all the overall State winner needs to do, is ask. The executive governor would sign all the requests with immediate effect.

'Banwo toured the city and when it was time to make his request, he opened his mouth and said:

"I request that children with and without chronic illness be protected from bullying in their school by an active and special anti-bullying policy."

The governor signed this into law immediately. Surprisingly, when the governor found out about Banwo's Dad, his humanitarian work as a Lieutenant in the Fire service of the State, he promoted David Banjoko to the post of District Chief of the fire service Centre, Ikeja. 'Banwo's Dad thus led the Year's National heroes' days ahead of many senior captains of the Fire Service Department in the same year of his only son's incredible conquest.

***

Three years post winning the State competition, 'Banwo stood at the entrance of the State University of Technology, Yaba, as a fresh undergraduate with a 100-per cent normal medical report; he has been seizure-free for more than 2 years and his anti-seizure medications had been discontinued by his neurologist. Undeniably, the Banjokos had a special Christmas that year.

While 'Banwo was decorating the Christmas tree that stood tall close to their Altar at home, he kept admiring the unwavering red light flickering close to the Sacred Heart of Jesus' icon. When 'Banwo closed his eyes this time around in gratitude, he could hear from the Dad's room a chorus so unmistaken in Mr Banjoko's baritone:

"Jingle bells, Jingle bells, jingle all the way, oh what fun it is to ride in a one-horse open sleigh…"

And when he opened his eyes, his mother kept her gaze on the Madonna embracing the Baby Jesus at their little Christmas Crib. Well, if she had not learnt anything, Mrs Banjoko knew that she could not care alone for all her son's needs; with her son's faith becoming her inspiration for the future, she echoed in awe: Truly: "OLUWABAMIWO Omo mi": 'BANWO: The LORD is helping me to look after my child!

EEG* - Electroencephalogram (A test or record that captures the electrical activity of the brain)

Everyday should be Christmas

by Obiora Oji

You know it is December when Daddy's tyres kick up clouds of brown dust as he drives off, and school suddenly becomes a happy place. Ibe starts to answer more to his other name – John Bull. He stops avoiding the teachers who insist on calling him by the 'English' name or chasing the friends who taunt him by making it even shorter.

Before the leaves dried out and the ground became harder, it was easy to spot Ibe chasing Charlie or David down the field. He ran after them like a bull – the Bull they teasingly called him. In his class, he was the only person who insisted that everyone should call him by his native name, at least, until December.

Everybody became friends as the year wrapped up. There were no more bright pupils but just pupils. Ibe oversaw the End of Year songs and dances. His friend, Ogo, was responsible for class decorations. For this last week in school, everyone was in charge of something.

Beautiful Aunty Claire supervised all her little managers. They were all done with the end-of-year examination and the teachers had finished marking their scripts. It was so difficult to tell what these young ones would become. She could guess. She had observed them all year. Why don't you ask them? She thought.
"Children!" She bellowed. Her voice cut out every other banter.

"Yes, Aunty!" They sang in unison.
"Hands   -on   your   neighbour's   - shoulders…straight!"
It was a drill they all knew too well. In one quick shuffle, fifteen pairs of hands lined up in brilliant order. Ibe was in front. He was a born leader, Miss Claire thought to herself.
"Shall we play a game?"
"Yes!" They chorused.
"What will you love to be when you grow up?"
        Many hands went up in the air.
"Shall we start from the back? Anita?"

***

'Roses in the garden. The green leaves are growing. Our love for you…shall never, never die.'

Ibe opened his eyes and smiled at the music. He had memorised the lyrics after dancing to it many times at the rehearsal. His dreams did not blur the words of the song. He wondered what time it was. He had slept off while questioning his answers to Miss Claire's question.
'Doctor,' he replied. What he didn't say was that he strictly wanted to be a village doctor – no more, no less. The holiday was coming and so were his uncles and aunts with their baggage of cousins.

Every year he stood under their shadows. He marvelled secretly at the tales of cinemas, the beauty of traffic lights, and the best of it all – the fast foods!

By the second day, Ibe would have taken centre stage. Last year, he took Dean and Phil to the stream. It was their first visit to the village, and after spending the first week getting introduced to resident kith and kin, they were desperate for their adventures.

'You wouldn't mind showing us the stream. Would you? Dean asked Ibe.

'Of course,' Ibe always found their mannerism very tricky. His Dad said the British spoke tongue in cheek.

He had quickly adjusted. Words were just words. When he replied 'of course,' he too was not sure if he had consented or not.

Dean and Phil had let out an excited yell. So it was game on!

The pathway to the stream had never seen a more enthusiastic trio. They chanted down the slopes, each clutching a small gallon. Ibe's Mum would never let them visit the stream and return empty-handed. The Briticos kept greeting everyone as they passed. Ibe had told them stories of monkeys that came to help humans with their laundry or to lift heavy containers on their heads. The wild fruits were quick to spot but the monkeys – not so much.

Ibe had prepared. His other village friends had been instructed to wear monkey costumes and to call out to the visitors from trees at a distance.

'Deeean,'

He froze. 'That's my name,' he said to no one in particular. He was scared.

'I think I know who that is.' Ibe said drawing Dean closer to him. 'If we stick together, Mowe – the wizard monkey – will not attack us.

'Attack us?' Both boys echoed at once. This was not part of Ibe's enticing tales.

'Let's walk on. Hand in Hand,' Ibe instructed.

As they bent round different bushes, they could hear rustlings and sometimes whispers of their names in no particular order.

In the end, they returned home. Hand in hand without water in their gallons.

The story of the "talking monkeys" would be told beyond the tiny village. Ibe was sure. When daylight whispered, Ibe opened his eyes. He was surprised that he had fallen asleep again. It was one week to Christmas. Seven days of magic.

Mama Ibe owned these last days. There was a routine faithfully followed every year. This year, Ibe did not hear the bargaining. Daddy always tried to price down the list his wife made.

'Ibeneme!' His Mum called. He ran towards the voice.

'You are still sleeping?' she asked.

Ibe shook his head. Mama was already dressed and set to go.

'Biko(please) get ready,' she ordered. 'We are going to the market!'

Ibe was ecstatic. As much as he anticipated it, every year came with its special stream of joy!

'And tell your sister to get ready too,' Mama shouted after him as he walked away.

The buzz of the Main Market on the Monday before Christmas was everything.

The barrow pushers having the business day of their lives were a constant threat for women and children.

'Uzo! Uzo! Uzo!' The chant was already playing in his head.

Mama does a good job of keeping the kids out of harm way.

Every year there were usually one or two popular cloth brands.

Last year was "what else?" Ibe wondered what this year's own would be.

More than half of Monday will be spent testing clothes and haggling prices.

It was the season. They could as well stay all day.

The important thing was everyone had to return home merry. Mama made sure of it every Christmas.

Baba's secret

by Oluwaseyi Adebola

Once upon a time, there was an eight-year-old boy named Bolaji Adeoye who lived with his Daddy and Mummy in Lagos state, Nigeria. He was an only child yet well-behaved, kind, and adventurous. His Dad, Kola, was a very successful banker and his Mum, Sade, was a brilliant medical doctor.

They lived in Victoria Island, Lagos, in a very posh and wealthy neighbourhood. Bolaji loved Lagos because of how alive it always felt – the bright streetlights, somewhat noisy hawkers in traffic jams, and Afropop music that blared from shops and canteens statewide. More importantly, Bolaji loved Christmas and all the joys that came with it. As Christmas neared, his father let him in on some exciting news.

'We are going to the village this Christmas to visit Baba!' He boomed in his deep baritone voice.

Occasionally they would travel to their village in Ondo state to visit Baba, who was his paternal grandfather. Bolaji did not know if Baba had any other names. Everyone called him Baba. He was a tall, lean man with bushy white hair and a soft voice. He was very wise and caring. Whenever they were home for Christmas, lots of villagers would troop into Baba's house to help settle their domestic scuffles. They always seemed at peace after talking to him. Baba however had a secret. Bolaji would find out about it before the end of their visit. It was a secret like no other!

The Adeoyes travelled by road to their village two days before Christmas day. Bolaji loved travelling with his parents in their air-conditioned Landcruiser jeep. He loved looking out the windows to see the mud houses with thatched roofs. He would see young boys and girls with plastic buckets on their heads, as they returned from fetching water in the village river. He loved hearing the songs they sang as they walked home cheerfully.

E mi ti pon omi mi. O tutu, O dan
Se iwo ti pon omi re? Se o tutu. Se o dan?

They would chorus happily in Yoruba. Bolaji's dad told him they meant they had fetched water that was cold and clean and asked each other if their water was the same. It sounded more magical in Yoruba. His mum taught him Yoruba, their mother tongue from time to time. There was however something that made Bolaji a little sad about travelling away from Lagos for Christmas. He would not get to see Father Christmas at the children party organized by his school every end of the year. He told his parents about this. They apologized but promised they would do something to cheer him up. Father Christmas is all Bolaji grew up to know, not Santa Claus as Caucasians would say.

When they got to the village, they went straight to Baba's compound. Bolaji prostrated on the ground to greet him. This always made Baba happy.

'O ko dada'. Baba would say, meaning that Bolaji was a well brought up child. Hearing this always pleased his parents.

On Christmas day, Bolaji was shocked to see Father Christmas sitting outside Baba's compound with lots of gifts. He even gave Bolaji the toy car he had been dreaming about. Bolaji was a good boy with excellent grades at school so his parents gave him whatever present he asked for. Bolaji could not believe his eyes – Father Christmas came all the way to the village for him! This was his best Christmas present ever!

On the day Bolaji and his parents were going to return to Lagos. He rushed into Baba's room to bid him farewell. He found Father Christmas' clothes hanging in the wardrobe. Did this mean his grandpa was Father Christmas? The famous Santa Claus that visited nice children all over the world to give them gifts? Grandpa asked Bolaji to keep it their little secret. He did not even tell his parents. It was not nice to reveal secrets people asked you not to share.

Bolaji returned to school the following year with a new swagger in his steps. He was a special child. He knew Baba's secret.

Moonlight Christmas

by Victoria Ozidu

The night was cold and the air full of strange creepy sounds but Chinelo had never felt more content or safe. Nestled in her father's arms, she felt as if she were in a warm soft bed instead of bare earth. She looked around at her elder brother, eleven and carefree, who was laughing and poking her elder sister, thirteen in the stomach.

Her sister Adanna stood up and began to chase him for daring to harass her. She turned her head towards the left and saw her mother who was busily stirring a pot of something. She wasn't sure what it was, but it smelled good. She still looked wan but at least she was better. They were not so afraid that she was going to leave them as they had been weeks ago. By her father's knee was her six-year-old friend Ogechi who was concentrating intently on plucking insects from the ground in front of her.

They called her a baby because she was the youngest, but at seven she knew she was no longer a baby. More so because she knew that her family had gone through a lot this year.

It had all started with something about land, her father said. She didn't understand fully but it seemed as if her father was about to lose his land. She had seen men in dark suits come and go, spouting words she couldn't understand, with ominous looks on their faces.

She had seen her father gnaw his nails in worry every evening when he returned from the farm and her mother's spirits droop, like a wilted flower. She no longer sang to them at night or in the early morning while making breakfast. Her sister and brother had also gone about their businesses with grave looks on their faces.

She had puzzled over it. She had asked them why they were sad, but they patted her head and told her not to worry. She later found out why they were sad when two months ago, the suits came in the early morning. This time they looked angry. They were shouting at father. Quietly, her mother and her siblings packed their clothing and a few household items. When they left the house, Chinelo knew they wouldn't come back.

They walked with their meagre possessions, passing other farms and houses until they got to the town's outskirts and it was there their father erected their present thatched shelter. Two days after they moved, mother cried in her sleep. Blood seemed to ebb out of her body. Her aunt had come to stay and help the family for a few days and Chinelo dimly understood that she had lost a possible younger brother; for it was a brother she wanted. Mother was dangerously sick for a few days and father looked older than ever and gnawed his nails harder. Adanna tried to behave like a grown woman as her mother recuperated. That had been nearly a month ago.

"Food is ready," her mother called out. They were all outside the tent. Chinelo stirred in her father's arms. Chijioke rushed to where the pot was as if he was afraid he wouldn't get his share. Mother ladled the soup into plates and Adanna set it out, placing the big bowl with wraps of fufu in the centre. It all seemed so familiar, like Christmases past.
Her father smiled benevolently and looked around at his family.

"Let us pray," he said with his head bowed. He was about to bless the food then he seemed to change his mind. He looked at the seven-year-old in his arms. "Chinelo, you pray for us."
"God, thank you for this food," Chinelo said. "Thank you for papa, mama, Ada, and

Chijioke. Thank you for Christmas. In Jesus name." The rest of the family boomed a loud 'Amen.'

As soon as she was through, she opened her eyes and saw that the night was bright. It was as if the moon had suddenly come out from where it was hiding, announcing the birth of the Saviour to them all.

"It's so bright," Ada said in awe.

"It's a full moon. We should dance," Chijioke said and proceeded to do a little jig on the spot. Her father smiled as lifted her from his lap and placed her on the ground, food momentarily forgotten. "It is usually maidens that dance at the full moon," he said.

"Now I want my two maidens Ada and Chinelo to dance for me. Ogechi will join them too. I and Chijioke will do the drumming."

His wife stood up. "I will join them too. They are small girls; they do not know how to dance."

"Mama, you will see something today," Ada said nodding her head confidently and began to sway from side to side.

Chinelo giggled and shook her tiny waist as her father and brother drummed on an empty pot. She had never had a more perfect

Christmas. The moon shined brighter still as if in agreement.

<u>*Bueno Christmas by Ejiro Eyaru*</u>

This Christmas is different from all the other Christmases I have had in my life. It is a good one; *Bueno* like Uncle Boniface said they say in Spain. I believe it is good because mama has said I do not have to work today and for the first time in my life I have received a Christmas present. One that I would cherish for the rest of my life.

My name is Godswill. I am the fifth in a family of six children. Our family lived in a rickety building in a compound with two rooms where we ate the daily bread of struggle. As the fifth child, I was neither special nor unwanted. I was just another mouth to feed.

Dad was a truck pusher and barely made enough to afford a meal at night. Mum hawked food during the day while we went to the nearby primary school which was free then. School was fun but I did not learn much as we did not really have any learning materials or even desks, but it was a way to pass the time.

Most of the children in my school seemed to come from a similar background as mine. I can only remember owning a pair of shoes once in my eleven years of age when an aunt came to visit and gave all of us shoes. I have since outgrown them.

Tragedy struck my family very early. My dad died after he was hit by a car while pushing his truck. There was no justice as the driver had run off. Life was already hard, but it got even harder. Mum told my older brothers and sister that they would have to fend for themselves and so sent them off to work for relatives. I was not surprised when Mum told me that I would have to leave school and join her in hawking.

Hawking was a hard job. It required patience, endurance, and stamina; something I did not have a lot of. Standing in the sun and walking for hours on end, ignoring jeers from would-be customers or other children, praying and hoping for someone to stop me so they could buy my wares was hardly my idea of fun.

But I quickly realized where my target customers were – in the primary school. Teachers and students alike usually got hungry around lunchtime, and I was a welcomed solution. Instead of walking around in the morning to other places to find customers, I began spending most of my time at the school wandering through the classes with my wares on my head. That was when I met Uncle Boniface.

Uncle Boniface was different from any teacher I had ever known. He seemed to have an interest in what he was teaching, and I was surprised when I saw students laughing in his class. He told them the importance of books. I soon learnt some of his favourite sayings;

"Readers are leaders. If you read, you will lead."

One day, Uncle Boniface noticed me at the window listening to him and asked me to come inside. I was so shy and shook my head, but he insisted. I cannot explain why I did it, but I ran away. I avoided his classes for some days after that incident. But that did not last long. His classes seemed to draw me in like a magnet. One morning, I was walking towards the school area with my wares on my head when I felt a hand on my arm. It was Uncle Boniface!

"Hey, are you not the one who has been standing at the window during my classes?" he asked, smiling kindly.

I nodded dumbly, not knowing what to say. I hoped he would not ban me from going to his classes.

"Ok look, standing at the window is not going to get you much of an education. We have got to do a bit more than that. Would you like to learn how to read?"

"Yes sir!" I said excitedly. At that moment, there was nothing else I would rather do.

Uncle Boniface then arranged to meet me for an hour after school where he began teaching me to read and write. He said I was very bright and before I knew it, I was learning quite a lot from him, and I enjoyed it. Thankfully, mama did not suspect anything as I was still able to sell all my wares by the end of the day. However, one day, Uncle Boniface said something that changed the course of my life.

"Godswill, I think you are very bright. You deserve to go to school. I want you to write the common entrance exam so you can go to secondary school. I felt apprehensive about this because for me to write the exam, I needed a parent's approval. Mama knew nothing about my time with Uncle Boniface. I was not sure she would understand as she had not gone to school herself. I need not have worried.

After a talk with Uncle Boniface, she smiled and told him: "I've noticed that Godswill has become happier now since his father died. Whatever will help him go further in life, I would not stop him."

She even gave me some time off from hawking to prepare for the exams. I was overjoyed when I discovered I had not only passed the exams, but I had won a scholarship that would run throughout secondary school. Uncle Boniface decided to buy me my very first present just before Christmas which was a collection of short stories. I would be going off to school at the beginning of the following year. I never had a book of my own and I knew without a doubt that this was one gift I would forever treasure. But I realized that what I cherished, even more than the book, was the fact that someone believed in me. And that is what made this Christmas the best I have ever had.

Akin's Christmas
by Jinmi Adetutu

It was 5:30 pm. Akin had just arrived home from boarding school where he had been for the first term of his first year in high school. Jingle Bell tunes were blasting from the Christmas lights hung around the street electricity poles with carnival posters draping from the lights.

The street was awash with the colours red and green as people attempted to decorate while almost every street corner had a fireworks hawker. Kids ran around with fireworks lights and adults were seen gathering around the live chicken stalls.

Akin's parents had left him in school for an extra day after the school closed for the session. He and two of his friends, Bola and Tunde, had a whole table to themselves that night. The food meant for 14 people was eaten by the 3 boys in minutes, each talking excitedly about their plans for Christmas and how they wanted the latest PS5 and just wanted to watch movies.

Akin was gisting his friends about how his Mum always made him watch the movie 'Jesus of Nazareth part 1, 2, and 3' every Christmas eve. He had watched it every year that even now, he was kind of looking forward to it.
Now sitting to have his dinner on his first night back, his Dad was going through his report card. "Akinola, how come you came 5th in your class this first term?"

"Dad, it was a difficult term. I did not resume school until after the mid-terms as I was in St Antonio's befo…"

"Young man, this sounds like loads of excuses. When I was your age, I was always first! I was never second."

"But Grandma said you started school at 12…." Akin's words faltered at the look his Dad gave him. He knew he was in trouble. Just at the right time, his Dad's phone rang, and Dad had to excuse himself to go receive the call.

Akin's younger sister came into the room. Tola was just 7 years old but was tall for her age.

"Akin, let's go and buy fireworks."

Akin knew he should not be buying such, but he was already angry at being shouted at and decided to be naughty. He still had some pocket money left from school and felt no one will know if they bought fireworks and kept them hidden in his school box.

The road was bustling, and everyone was lighting their fireworks. The sky was very colourful, making Tola and Akin spend time watching the well-lit sky. Bola had just gotten one Spangler and thought he'd try to scare

Akin. He threw the firework in Akin's direction, thinking everyone will run as usual. Unfortunately, Akin and Tola were distracted by the sky and did not know until it was too late. A loud bang... 'GBOOOOOS'.

Akin jerked awake. It was all a dream. He had been sleeping and dreaming. His friends had just come into the dormitory and were laughing and shouting. It was the last night of the term and he was due to get his report card tomorrow. "God, please let me not be 5th, let me not be 5th" he silently prayed.

His Mum was coming to pick him up from school tomorrow and they will be travelling to the United Kingdom for Christmas. Dad had recently moved there after getting a job as a doctor and he was looking forward to the trip. His friends have asked him to take pictures of the London Eye, the London Bridge and of the plane when he took off.

***

He turned to sleep but could not sleep again. His parents had promised him a jolly good vacation if he made it to the top three in his class. His dad had joked that his passport was kept at the embassy and the officials will not release it and allow him to travel if he did not have a good result.

Dad had also told him how UK's Santa Claus was slightly different from the Father Christmas they saw as kids. The Santa Claus in the UK came down the chimney and had a list of all kids who were good and bad. He gave good presents to the good kids and the bad ones, well… they received nothing. You also had to leave out cookies and milk for Santa and his reindeer.

All Akin could think of now was all the mistakes he had made this year; he had misplaced his keys the first week of arriving at the boarding school. Most of his cutleries were missing and he tore one of his shorts while playing soccer with Bola and Tunde, and now, he was not sure he was going to make the 'good boy' list of Santa Claus. While pondering all these, the morning bell rang; it was the last day of school.

***

His Mum showed up early with his sister, Tola, to pick him. He had just received his report card and came 3rd in his class! "Now, the UK officials have no excuse for keeping my passport, I get to travel. Yippee!". His Mum started laughing. "Akin, your passport has been with me for about 2 weeks now. We have bought your tickets and we are all travelling." Tola and Akin started shouting and singing in the car; they were going to the United Kingdom at last.

Akin had a hurried dinner. He was too excited to stay still. He face-timed his friends and they all chatted about their first evening back. Everyone talked about their results and who had come first and who had not done so well. Bola made a funny statement and laughed about a girl that came last. It seemed to have rubbed Akin the wrong way "Bola, but I am not sure that is funny, after all, Tinuke came first."

"Akin, of course, I was not laughing because she is a girl…"
"I have to leave now as my Mum is calling me". Akin was sad because he understood that mocking people wasn't a good idea. He knew his friends to be good guys and was surprised Bola felt the need to go there. Mum had

instilled in him the need not to gossip as it was not a good thing to do.

The voice of his Mum startled him out of his reverie, "Akin, come and put your school uniforms in the laundry and start packing your box." It was truly happening; they were going to the UK.

The next morning dawned bright and early. There was a chill in the air and everywhere appeared white. It was foggy and cold in Lagos. Akin ran to the car to retrieve one of the novels that he left in the car. He was looking forward to finishing the first instalment of the Harry Potter series on the plane. While outside, he saw his neighbour, Mr Saka, cleaning his car. Mr Saka will drive them to the airport later that evening.

"Good morning Mr Saka.

"Akin, good morning. How was your journey home?"

"Fine sir. What of Tobi?" Tobi was Mr Saka's son and was Akin's age mate but he attended another school.

"Tobi went out with his Mum early this morning."

Akin picked his novel and went inside. It was time for morning prayers and mum asked Akin to pray. He was still worried that all the promise of travel was an expensive joke by his Mum. He asked to see the passports so he could see the visas stamped in them. "Akin, you have to be able to focus and learn to commit things to God even when you are super excited. I am excited too, but when it is time to pray, it is not time to be distracted. And the passports are not running away. Now pray young man!" his Mum scolded him.

Was this going to count as a bad deed for him? Will he be missing Santa's gift this year? He knew Santa was not real but what if it was real in the UK and not in Nigeria? His dad had shown him an app that tracked Santa's movement on Christmas eve. With these thoughts, he started praying and asked for forgiveness of sin.

It was 5 pm and it was time to leave for the airport. The flight was for 10 pm but Mum was worried that if they did not leave now, they might get stuck on 3rd Mainland Bridge traffic. The bridge was the second-longest bridge in Africa, the first being the 6th October Bridge in

Egypt. Akin smiled to himself – he still remembered his social studies.

The traffic was however moving so slowly. This is what is called hold up or standstill. We have not moved for the last 30 mins!". Fear started to creep in: was he going to miss his flights and not get to travel? He had amazing plans to play in the snow and to take pictures.

This holiday was not going to end before it even started. Bowing his head, he said a word of prayer. Their car eventually started moving as Mr Saka found ways to navigate the car forward. He kept praying while his Mum looked on in surprise. His younger sister was playing video games and did not seem as bothered.

With 30 mins to spare, they made it to the airport. There was a dash through check-in and immigration. As they ran towards the gates, they heard an announcement on the loudspeaker: 'This is an announcement that Nigeria Airways Flight 104 has been delayed…' Akin was so pent up he screamed "noooooooohhhh" '… by approximately 10 mins' "Yaay, it is just 10 mins!" he shouted with his sister.

They were then able to relax and walk to the gate. Before he knew it, he was on-board the aircraft and fastening his seat belt. He was really travelling for Christmas!!! The captain came on and talked about the flight. Within a few minutes, the plane was taxiing for take-off. Grabbing onto Tola's hand on his left and his Mum's hand on the right, the plane took off into the sky. Everything was right with the world and Akin was travelling for Christmas.

<u>BIOGRAPHIES OF AUTHORS</u>

Dr. Ejiro Eyaru is a General Practitioner who is an avid lover of African stories. He writes poetry in his spare time and has recently taken to writing his own stories. He is married to the love of his life Dena and they have two children.

Dr. Oluwaseyi Adebola (MBBS Ilorin; MSc Translational Neuropathology, Sheffield) is the author of "A Cluster of Petals," a collection of short stories shortlisted for the 2019 Quraimo Writers Prize and the 2019 AFIRE Linda Ikeji prize for Literature. He is also the founder of CreativeNaija.com, a social network for Creative Nigerians. Seyi is married to Funmi and their union is blessed with the most beautiful boy in the world, 'Tise. Follow him on Twitter @laylow1388

Dr. Adebola Adisa is a General Practitioner and speaker. She is a school governor, STEM Ambassador and Black Women in Health (BWIH) executive. Dr. Adisa is the founder of Brave Hearts, a charity which supports her community. She has authored 5 other books; The Magic of Destiny, Be inspired, Kaleidoscopes, How to Write Your Book 101 and a Children's book, Dr Facts Continents of the World. She stays active through gardening and enjoys spending time with her family.

Emmanuel Onimisi is a Creative writer, artist, and environmental researcher. He writes poetry and speculative fiction, and is the Author of Portal and The Curious Case of Doctor Maundy. He loves music, stories, comics and the simplification of complexities in teaching.

Dr. Victoria Olasegha is a psychiatrist, business woman and creative writer. She has written and published several books including ' Bedazzled', 'Overcoming the Odds' and 'The Journey's End.' You can find her literary works as well as her blog on vickyseghasworld.com. She is also known as Victoria Ozidu on some of her works.

Leke Amoo is a passionate teacher, school leader and writer. He Authored the Smart Book for Smart Parents and runs the blog www.penspeakers.com. When he's not teaching or writing, he's either tickling his daughter or being tickled by his wife.

Dr KAYODE, Olamide Sinmidele Valentine (MBBS Ogb. PGPN, Boston Sch.of Med; FWACP Paed; FMCPaed) is an intrepid and award - winning Child's Specialist, an illustrious Nigerian Author of five literary works and other multiple academic works in Paediatrics. His creative writings speak courage, resilience and diligence in Pearls and Pebbles 1 and 2; The Void, ÈJÌRÉ ALÀDÚKÈ and Mothering without Murdering. Dr Kayode is the convener of Paediatrics - online - a platform for mentoring and teaching medical students; his love for music and family life is exceptional.

Dr. Obiora Oji- Nigerian born, part Nigerian part UK trained GP is the self-acclaimed Duke of NDUK (Nigerian Doctors in the UK). He is the author of 'To Err is Woman' and the Director of CleanPay- a tech for solution start-up. Among his many passions, serial entrepreneurship resonates most with him

Dr. Funom Theophilus Makama is a medical doctor, a political activist, a poet and a public health enthusiast. As a writer, he has authored 10 books and co-Authored 2 more. Among his successful books are: Tropical 20,000, the medical textbook series in Paediatrics, Surgery, Obs & Gyn and Internal Medicine; The Soul Talkers, The Bastard Citizen, The Devil's orchid, Biblical Love Psychology and two political textbooks exposing the open-secret Agenda behind the killings and forcefully attempted aristocracy of one tribe on over 500 others in the Nigerian society. He is married to the most beautiful woman in the world and together, they have 3 children

Dr. Olujinmi Adetutu is a husband to an amazing wife and a father. He is a creative writer, performer and founding partner of Open Docs- a group of Nigeria-trained doctors in diaspora focused on improving healthcare delivery in Nigeria.

Dr. Niyi Marcus is a General Practitioner. He lives and works in England. He enjoys poetry, photography and karaokeing in his spare time

Printed in Great Britain
by Amazon

11205594R00088